P9-DVI-928

T 159809

VISTA GRANDE
PUBLIC LIBRARY

© 2007 Disney Enterprises, Inc. All rights reserved.

RADIO FLYER is a registered trademark of Radio Flyer, Inc. and is used with permission.

Published by Scholastic Inc., 90 Old Sherman Turnpike, Danbury, Connecticut 06816.

No part of this publication may be reproduced in whole or in part, or stored in a retrieval
system, or transmitted in any form or by any means, electronic, mechanical, photocopying,
recording, or otherwise, without written permission of the copyright holder.

SCHOLASTIC and associated logos are trademarks and/or registered
trademarks of Scholastic Inc.

For information regarding permission, write to:
Disney Licensed Publishing, 114 Fifth Avenue, New York, New York 10011.

978-0-439-02414-3
0-439-02414-5

Printed in the U.S.A.
First printing, May 2007

WALT DISNEY
PICTURES PRESENTS

MEET THE ROBINSONS

SCHOLASTIC INC.
New York   Toronto   London   Auckland   Sydney
Mexico City   New Delhi   Hong Kong   Buenos Aires

On a cold, rainy night, a lone figure laid a box at the door of the 6th Street orphanage and ran away.

Mildred, the kindly orphanage director, heard a knock and slowly opened the door.

Nearly 13 years later, that baby had grown into a young inventor named Lewis. But Lewis couldn't invent the thing he wanted most: a family.

One day, Lewis demonstrated his latest device to a couple he hoped would adopt him. But the Peanut-Butter-and-Jelly Sandwich Maker exploded all over everything!

Lewis was so disappointed. He wished his real mother were there. He decided to find a way to remember her. He set to work creating a device called a Memory Scanner, which, Lewis hoped, would be able to recall memories from the past.

Lewis worked many nights on the invention, keeping awake his poor roommate, Mike "Goob" Yagoobian.

Finally, Lewis finished the Memory Scanner and entered it in the school science fair.

On the big day, the school gym was bustling with excitement. Dr. Krunklehorn, a real scientist from Inventco Labs, was one of the judges. An anxious Lewis placed his invention on the table and covered the device with a blanket.

Suddenly a boy named Wilbur Robinson
magically appeared. Wilbur said he was from
the future! Wilbur asked Lewis if he had seen
a tall man in a bowler hat, who Wilbur explained,
had stolen a Time Machine.

Little did the boys know that Bowler Hat Guy was hiding nearby! His evil partner, a robotic bowler hat named Doris, quietly uncovered Lewis's Memory Scanner. With a steely claw, Doris loosened the Memory Scanner bolts, and tore off a bracket. She then slipped away unnoticed.

Finally, Lewis presented the Memory Scanner to the judges. With a whir, the device sprang to life. Then it started to shake. The fan flew off, smashing the ceiling lights. One thing led to another, and soon the entire gym was in chaos!

With tears in his eyes, Lewis ran back to the orphanage and climbed up to the roof where he ripped out pages from his invention notebook.

Then Wilbur appeared again. "Coo, coo" he said, pretending to be a pigeon. Wilbur insisted that Lewis fix his Memory Scanner. To prove he was from the future, Wilbur pushed an unsuspecting Lewis into his Time Machine.

"To the future!" said Wilbur, as they blasted off. Lewis's eyes grew wide as he stared out the window of Wilbur's Time Machine. The future looked amazing!

Wilbur kept talking about fixing the Memory Scanner. But all Lewis wanted to do was use the Time Machine to go back and see his mother. After tearing up the Memory Scanner plans, Lewis grabbed the controls of the Time Machine. The boys scuffled and ended up crash-landing not far from Wilbur's house.

Meanwhile, Bowler Hat Guy was still in the present. He attempted to pass off the Memory Scanner as his own invention at Inventco headquarters. But Bowler Hat Guy didn't know how to turn on the device! The Inventco chairman threw him out.

Bowler Hat Guy looked at Doris and said, "We must find that boy!"

Back in the future, Wilbur and Lewis pushed the damaged Time Machine into the Robinson's garage. Lewis agreed to try to fix the Time Machine if Wilbur would take him to the past to see his mother.

Wilbur put a silly fruit hat on Lewis's head to disguise his hair and ordered him not to leave the garage.

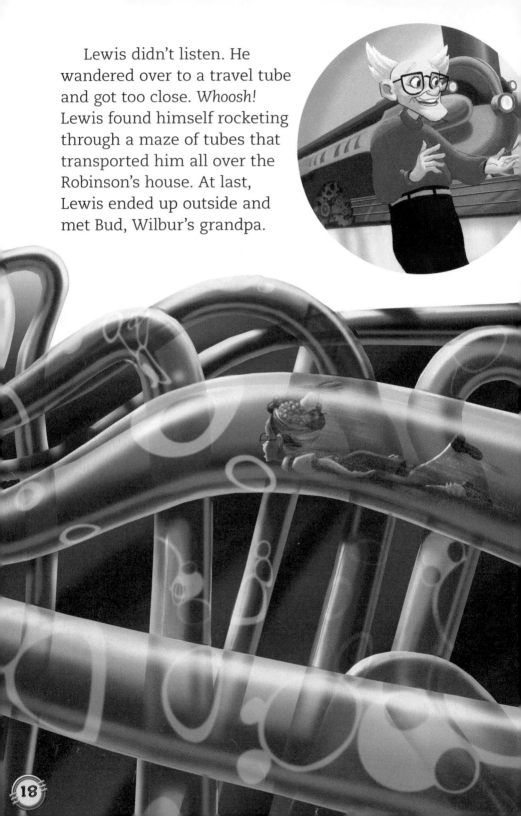

Lewis didn't listen. He wandered over to a travel tube and got too close. *Whoosh!* Lewis found himself rocketing through a maze of tubes that transported him all over the Robinson's house. At last, Lewis ended up outside and met Bud, Wilbur's grandpa.

Together, Lewis and Grandpa took the tubes
to every room in the house; and Lewis met nearly all
of the Robinsons, including Uncle Gaston, the human
cannonball; Uncle Art, an intergalactic pizza delivery
guy; cousin Tallulah, who wore a skyscraper headpiece;
Uncle Fritz and his wife, Petunia, a hand puppet; and
cousin Laszlo, whose propeller helmet helps him fly.

Wilbur was furious when he found Lewis. "I told you to stay in the garage!"

"I did," said Lewis. "But I went up the tube, and I ran into your family and—"

Wilbur panicked. Luckily, no one had realized Lewis was from the past.

Back at the orphanage, Bowler Hat Guy was looking for Lewis. But he only found Goob, Lewis's roommate.

Goob had been beaten up by his teammates after missing the game-winning catch and losing the championship. Bowler Hat Guy encouraged Goob to keep his bitter feelings inside.

In the future, Wilbur told Lewis about his inventor father, Cornelius Robinson. The world knew Cornelius as the "Founder of the Future." Wilbur explained that when his father failed (like when he invented Doris, originally intended as a helpful hat), he learned from those mistakes. Cornelius's motto was "keep moving forward."

That story inspired Lewis. The boy tried to fix the broken Time Machine, but he failed.

Just then Franny, Wilbur's mother, called the boys to dinner. The Robinsons were having spaghetti and meatballs. Uncle Gaston was even shooting meatballs from one of the cannons he invented!

At the same time, Bowler Hat Guy and Doris had just arrived in the stolen Time Machine. Bowler Hat Guy had gone back in time to steal a dinosaur to help kidnap Lewis. Controlled by a Little Doris on his head, the T-rex crashed through the Robinson's dining room and chased Lewis.

The entire family sprang into action. Wilbur launched a meatball using Uncle Gaston's cannon. It ricocheted off a wall and knocked Little Doris off the dino's head.

Bowler Hat Guy lost control of the beast! The T-rex stopped chasing Lewis. He was safe!

The Robinsons and their robot, Carl, gathered around Lewis. Everyone agreed that he was a wonderful boy, who deserved to have a family that loved him.

"Lewis, do you want to be a Robinson?" Franny asked.

Lewis couldn't believe what he was hearing. But Wilbur knew better. He knocked the hat off Lewis's head. The Robinsons gasped when they saw Lewis's hair and realized that he was from the past. Franny told Lewis he would have to return to his own time. Worst of all, Wilbur said he never intended on taking him back in time to find his mom.

Feeling betrayed, Lewis ran away.

But the ever-resourceful Bowler Hat Guy found Lewis and promised to take the boy to see his mother. In return, Lewis agreed to show Bowler Hat Guy how to turn on the Memory Scanner.

In a dank, dark room, Lewis turned on the Memory Scanner. Bowler Hat Guy then tied Lewis up and switched on a light to reveal that they were in the old orphanage.

The light illuminated another surprise. Bowler Hat Guy was someone Lewis knew very well. . . .

"Yes, it is I! Mike Yagoobian," said the wiry villain. "If you hadn't kept me up all night working on your stupid project, then I wouldn't have missed the catch. Eventually, they closed down the orphanage and everyone left, except me."

Bowler Hat Guy had stolen the Time Machine in the future to get his revenge on Lewis and ruin the course of his life. Lewis suddenly realized something even more shocking. He would grow up to be the inventor, Cornelius Robinson, Wilbur's father!

Bowler Hat Guy took Lewis and the Memory Scanner to the roof, where Bowler Hat Guy had parked the stolen Time Machine.

Luckily, help was on the way! To Lewis's surprise, Wilbur and Carl rescued him from the villain.

Bowler Hat Guy, who still had the Memory Scanner, blasted off in his Time Machine, landing in the present. At Inventco, Bowler Hat Guy convinced the chairman to purchase the Memory Scanner. If that happened, he would change the future! Lewis's future as a famous inventor would never come to pass.

As Wilbur pleaded with Lewis to fix the Time Machine, the boys heard a strange rushing noise. Suddenly Wilbur was pulled into the darkening sky.

"Wilbur!" shouted Lewis. But in the future that Bowler Hat Guy had created, Wilbur didn't exist.

Lewis knew he had to work quickly to restore
things to the way they had been. Working hard, he
made a final adjustment to Wilbur's broken Time
Machine and successfully started the vehicle.

Lewis punched a date into the Time Machine's dashboard control. *Whrrrr!* The Time Machine transported Lewis back in time to Inventco's headquarters.

"Goob, stop!" Lewis commanded, "She's using you Goob, and once she gets what she wants she'll get rid of you." When he saw Doris, Lewis made a promise never to invent her, and with that, she instantly disappeared.

Lewis and Bowler Hat Guy zoomed away from Inventco and returned to the future to find it completely restored. The sun grew brighter, as they landed at the Robinson's house. And Wilbur had returned!

When Wilbur saw Bowler Hat Guy, he ran to tackle him. "He's the bad guy!" yelled Wilbur.

"No, he's not," said Lewis. "He's my roommate."

As the two boys talked, Bowler Hat Guy quietly slipped away. He had decided it was time for him to find his own way in the future.

Just then Cornelius Robinson arrived home and met Lewis.

"Wowee!" said Lewis. "So if I go back now, then this will be my future?"

"That depends on you," said Cornelius. "You've got to make the right choices and keep moving forward."

Lewis waved good-bye to the Robinsons.

Wilbur kept his promise to take Lewis back in time to see his mother. This was the chance Lewis had been waiting for all of his life. But he knew he had to move forward and live the life that was waiting for him. So Lewis got back into the Time Machine.

Wilbur brought Lewis back to the present. But before returning to the science fair, Lewis raced to the baseball field.

"Goob! Wake up!" he yelled across the fence.
And with that, sleepy little Goob yawned, stretched
out his glove—and made the game winning catch.
The crowd cheered. Goob was a hero!

GO DINOS

Lewis returned to the science fair and asked for a second chance to demonstrate his invention. Dr. Krunklehorn volunteered to test the Memory Scanner.

"Just give me a date to input," Lewis said, and she whispered in his ear. The Memory Scanner's screen began to flow, then it showed the image of Dr. Krunklehorn's wedding. The invention worked!

Dr. Krunklehorn was impressed. In fact, she and her husband, Bud Robinson, soon adopted Lewis and he changed Lewis's name to Cornelius.

Lewis finally had a family, and his future looked very, very bright.

EYE SPY

Take your own time machine back through the story and try to find the futuristic pictures.